Dear Rose and Kai,

Best wishes!

Jim Rumonda

3/6/2006

THE JAMES H W THOMPSON FOUNDATION

First published in Thailand in 2006 by The James H. W. Thompson Foundation

Distributed by

The James H. W. Thompson Foundation
6 Soi Kasemsan 2
Rama 1 Road, Bangkok, Thailand
Email: info@jimthompsonhouse.com
http//www.jimthompsonhouse.com

River Books Co., Ltd.
396 Maharaj Road, Tatien
Bangkok 10200
Tel: (66) 2 225 4963, 002 0139; 622 1900
Fax: (66) 2 225 3861
Email: riverps@ksc.th.com
www.riversbookssbk.com

Copyright collective work © The James H. W. Thompson Foundation 2006
Copyright text © Jane Puranananda 2006
Copyright illustrations © The James H. W. Thompson Foundation 2006

Illustrated by Camille Geslin
Edited by Bonnie Thalman
Production by Supicha Teerasenee

ISBN 974-94112-6-9

Bound and printed in Thailand by Sirivatana Interprint Public Co., Ltd.

THE MYSTERY OF THE
VANISHING VASE
AT THE JIM THOMPSON HOUSE

By Jane Puranananda
Illustrations by Camille Geslin

One Monday morning something strange happened at the Jim Thompson House in Bangkok. As usual, visitors from all over the world were waiting to go on a tour of the old wooden house that had been turned into a museum. Jim Thompson built the house a long time ago and decorated it with many beautiful art objects. He liked sharing his house with others, so he arranged for guides to take visitors on tours through the house.

On that day a nice guide named Miss Pim was leading the first tour around the house. When she brought the visitors into the dining room, she pointed to the dining table. The table was set for a meal with beautiful old Chinese plates, crystal glasses and colorful napkins.

Next Miss Pim drew attention to a tall Chinese table against the wall and said, "This old blue and white vase...." Then to her surprise, she noticed the large vase had vanished! She looked around. To her relief, she saw the missing vase sitting on a small cabinet.

"That is very strange," she thought. "The vase was on the high table yesterday. I wonder who moved it."

Later, when she finished the tour, Miss Pim went to see Mr. Wise, the museum director. She reported to him about the vanishing vase. The director went upstairs and very carefully moved the precious object back to where it belonged.

Mr. Wise asked all the guides about the vase, but no one knew who had moved it. He decided he would watch the house very carefully over the next few days to see if he could discover why this had happened. This was certainly a mystery!

That same week Eric and his sister Beatrice flew to Bangkok. They were traveling with their uncle, Dr. Burdley, who was a famous art expert. Dr. Burdley was going to Bangkok to study the art collection at the Jim Thompson House.

Eric and Beatrice had never been to Bangkok. Their school was closed for the summer holidays, so Dr. Burdley asked their parents if they could join him on his trip. The two young people were very excited about visiting Thailand. Traveling to Southeast Asia would be a great adventure. They planned to explore Bangkok while Dr. Burdley was working.

Bangkok

The following Monday morning, Dr. Burdley was standing with Beatrice and Eric in the garden of the Jim Thompson House. The museum director, Mr. Wise, introduced the three visitors to the guides.

"Guides, this is Dr. Burdley and his niece Beatrice and nephew Eric. Dr. Burdley is here to study the collection in our museum. He will be looking at the paintings, the ceramics and the other art objects in the house."

Suddenly Miss Pim rushed up. She had just finished the first guided tour of the house.

"The vase has been moved again!" she exclaimed. Then she told Mr. Wise that she found the vase in the wrong place, just like last Monday.

Mr. Wise, Dr. Burdley, Eric and Beatrice went upstairs with Miss Pim to the dining room to have a look.

Mr. Wise was surprised. "I am certain the vase was on the tall Chinese table when I locked the house last night. How could someone have moved it? The guard was here all night," he noted.

Everyone stood looking puzzled.

Finally, Mr. Wise said, "Who could have done this? This is very serious. The artwork in this house is old and valuable. It cannot be moved around without my permission. We must hire a detective. I want to know who is doing this!"

Eric turned and whispered to Beatrice, "Wow, a real mystery! I can solve this, and you are going to be my assistant. But you must keep our plans a secret."

"I won't tell," said Beatrice, "but I don't see how we can solve this mystery. We are not from here. We don't know anyone. What can we do?"

"Exactly," said Eric, "because we are not from here, we can ask lots of questions. Just get out your notepad and record the clues we find."

With that, Eric turned to Mr. Wise, "Excuse me, sir, would you mind telling us about Jim Thompson?"

Eric whispered to Beatrice, "I am sure we can find a clue to this mystery if we know something about Jim Thompson."

Eric asked Mr. Wise, "Exactly who was Jim Thompson, and what was he doing in Thailand? Did you know him?"

"I met Jim Thompson when I was a very young man and first came to Bangkok," replied the director. "He was an American who came to Thailand a long time ago. He liked Thailand very much and wanted to help the Thai people. He noticed that some Thais still wore traditional outfits made of silk. He thought people in other countries would like to buy this beautiful cloth, so he started a company to sell Thai silk. His idea was very successful, and his company is still in business today."

"Where does silk come from?" asked Beatrice.

"Silk comes from a special insect called a silkworm. In villages in many parts of Thailand, silkworms are raised for their silk. The worm must be cared for carefully and fed mulberry leaves. After about a month, the worm stops eating and begins to spin a cocoon. To obtain silk threads, the cocoon must be delicately unrolled. The silk threads are gathered in bunches and dyed different colors. After dyeing, they are dried in the sun and then rolled onto spools. Then the villagers use a special wooden machine called a 'loom' to weave the threads into cloth. Weaving silk takes a great deal of skill," explained Mr. Wise.

"Does this house have anything to do with Jim Thompson's silk business?" asked Eric.

"Oh, yes," said Mr. Wise. "Jim Thompson built his house right here so he could be near the silk weaving village on the other side of the canal." Mr. Wise pointed to a group of buildings across the water. "Jim Thompson used to visit the silk weavers every morning. He made them his partners."

"Where is Jim Thompson now?" asked Eric.

"Oh, he went on a vacation forty years ago and disappeared without a trace. His disappearance is still an unsolved mystery," said Mr. Wise. "But I am certain he would be happy to know that so many people enjoy visiting his house."

After Mr. Wise left, Eric told Beatrice to write in her notebook: "Solving the mystery of the blue and white vase. Point 1 - Jim Thompson built his house next to the silk weaving village. Point 2 - Anyone who knew Jim Thompson would be very old now. Point 3 - Jim Thompson disappeared a long time ago."

Beatrice looked puzzled, "I do not see what this has to do with solving the mystery," she said.

Eric just smiled and said, "You'll see. Little details are important."

The next day Beatrice and Eric came back to the house. They wanted to go on a tour with Miss Pim. While they waited for the tour, they talked to Mr. Wise.

"Has the detective come yet?" asked Eric.

"Oh, yes, he looked for fingerprints on the vase but he found nothing. The vase had been wiped clean. There was no trace of who touched it. I find this very strange," he replied.

Eric turned to Beatrice and said, "Point 4 - The vase had been wiped clean."

Just then Miss Pim came up and started the museum tour. She led the group into the house and up a flight of stairs. She pointed to the old paintings that lined the walls.

"These paintings tell the stories of the former lives of the Buddha, who was a great teacher. We believe he had 547 previous lives, and in each life he did a good deed. Most paintings in Thailand tell stories about his last ten lives. Here is one where he is a king riding on an elephant," said the guide.

15

Eric and Beatrice looked closely at the paintings and studied the one of the king riding on an elephant.

"Why is the elephant white?" asked Beatrice. The elephant she had seen in the zoo was gray.

"White elephants are considered to be very special. They are thought to bring good luck to the kingdom. So if a white elephant is found in the forest, it is presented to the king," explained Miss Pim.

Upstairs there was a lovely stone statue of a seated man. Beatrice heard one of the visitors whisper, "He is smiling so peacefully."

Miss Pim looked at the statue and said, "This is an image of the Buddha. He lived in India over two thousand years ago. He taught us the way to find happiness within ourselves."

Eric looked at Beatrice and said, "He looks so calm and very wise. I am sure he would know how to solve the mystery of the vanishing vase."

Next they walked into the dining room. Eric and Beatrice looked carefully at the mysterious blue and white vase to make sure it was in the right place. The vase was standing on the high Chinese table - exactly where it belonged.

"Do you think someone could have climbed in the window to move the vase?" asked Beatrice.

"Let's have a look," said Eric.

Then the two walked over to the window and looked outside.

"This house certainly has many rooms," said Beatrice.

"Yes," agreed Eric. He looked carefully at the windows and doors. He noticed they all had strong shutters which could be closed at night.

"With the shutters closed tightly at night, I do not think anyone could enter this house through a window," noted Eric.

From the dining room they walked into a large living room. Beatrice liked this room. It faced the garden. There were many wonderful decorations, including graceful wooden statues standing in openings in the wall.

Miss Pim explained that the openings used to be windows, but Jim Thompson turned them into display spaces. She said they could no longer be windows because he added rooms on either side of the living room.

"Interesting, hidden windows," said Eric. "I wonder what other secrets this house has."

After that they toured three more rooms - the study, the guestroom and Jim Thompson's own bedroom. At the end of the tour, Eric asked Miss Pim if she would mind answering a few more questions.

"Could you explain about how Jim Thompson built this house?" he asked.

"Certainly," she answered. "Jim Thompson bought some old wooden houses made of teak and had them moved to this site. He made a special plan and had all the different houses put together."

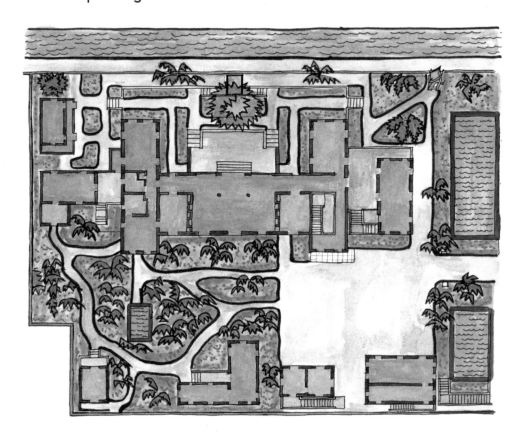

"What is teak?" asked Beatrice.

"Teak is a special kind of hardwood which is found in tropical rain forests. It takes a long time to grow. In the old days, people used to build their houses out of teak because it is strong. Elephants were used to move the heavy teak logs," replied Miss Pim.

She continued, "Old teak houses were built on stilts to protect people from flooding. They could easily be taken down and moved, if the flooding became too bad. To build this house, Jim Thompson searched for old teak houses. Some houses even came from the old weaving village across the canal."

After Miss Pim left, Eric asked Beatrice to write in the notebook, "Point 5 – Jim Thompson's house is made from old houses moved here, and some came from across the canal."

On Wednesday Beatrice and
Eric came to the museum to have
lunch with Dr. Burdley. While they
waited for him in the library, they looked through old books with pictures of the
museum. Suddenly Eric said to Beatrice, "This is very strange. In this old picture
the blue and white vase is on the small cabinet."

Just then Mr. Wise walked in and Eric asked him, "I thought the vase belonged on
the big table. Why is it on the small cabinet in this picture?"

"Oh, it used to be on the small cabinet when Jim Thompson lived here. We moved
it not long ago. We were afraid a visitor would bump into the cabinet, and it would
fall and break," said Mr. Wise.

Eric whispered to Beatrice, "Point 6 - The blue and white vase used to be on the
small cabinet when Jim Thompson lived in the house."

At lunch Eric asked his uncle about the vase, "Why is the vase so special? It looks like a big flowerpot to me."

Dr. Burdley answered, "That particular vase was made in China almost seven hundred years ago during a time called the Yuan dynasty. Over the years, the Chinese became famous for making the finest dishes and bowls in the world. They would load them into ships and send them off to be sold in distant countries. Many ships sank and hundreds of bowls and dishes were lost. Over the years many vases have broken, so they became rare and valuable. Today some treasure hunters search the bottom of the sea to find sunken ships with old vases."

"That means old vases and bowls are worth a lot of money," said Eric.

"Oh, yes," confirmed Dr. Burdley, "they are very valuable."

"Can you tell how old a vase is by looking at it?" asked Eric.

"Experts have spent years studying the shape, patterns and designs of vases. Old bowls and dishes are decorated with special styles of flowers, birds and animals. We also study the markings on the bottom of the dishes to tell how old they are," explained Dr. Burdley.

"Do the Chinese only make blue and white bowls?" asked Beatrice.

"Oh no, they make many other types, like the ones you saw in the glass cases in the room next to the dining room. Those colorful bowls and dishes are decorated in five colors with special Thai designs, but they also were made in China," continued Dr. Burdley.

"Are they valuable?" asked Beatrice.

"Extremely valuable," replied Dr. Burdley. "Originally those dishes were made to be used at the royal court. They are very special."

Then the children's uncle said, "Now I have a surprise for you. Tomorrow I will take you to the beach. We will come back here on Monday morning to say good-bye, and then we will go home."

After lunch Eric said, "Wow, if we are leaving for the beach, we have to work fast to solve the mystery. Let's look for clues in the garden."

The garden was filled with big trees and plants. When Eric and Beatrice stood in the middle, they could not see anything but leaves and bushes. Then Eric saw an old man sweeping leaves. He was the gardener.

"Excuse me, sir, could we ask you a few questions?" he asked. "Have you worked here a long time? Did you know Jim Thompson?"

At first Eric was afraid he did not understand, but slowly the gardener replied, "When I was a little boy, my father was Jim Thompson's gardener. I have worked here for a long time. There are very few people who worked for Mr. Jim who take care of the house today." He walked off before Eric could ask any more questions.

After the gardener left, Eric turned to Beatrice and said, "Point 7 - Very few people who worked for Jim take care of the house today."

"What does that mean? Do you think anyone else here besides Dr. Wise and the gardener knew Jim Thompson? They would be very old by now," said Beatrice.

"I am not sure, but somehow I think it is important," said Eric.

With that, the two continued to explore the rest of the garden. They walked past a beautiful statue wearing a long robe.

Beatrice paused for a moment in front of a stone figure. "I remember this statue from the book in the library. This is a very old image of the Buddha. I wish the head were not broken off so we could see his face," she commented.

They followed the path until they reached a small structure that looked like a dollhouse.

"This is a spirit house," Eric told Beatrice. "Uncle Burdley says they are built to apologize to the spirits who are disturbed when you build a new house. I wish the spirits could talk to us and tell us who has been moving the vase!"

Then suddenly Eric climbed into the thick bushes near the wall by the canal. He spotted a torn piece of soft white cloth stuck to a bush.

Eric climbed out of the bushes. He showed the torn cloth to Beatrice and said, "Point 8 – Soft white cloth found in bushes near the canal."

Just then Dr. Burdley called to Eric and Beatrice, "Time to go. We need to pack for the beach. We leave early tomorrow morning."

Eric ran up to his uncle saying, "Just one minute. I must give something to Miss Pim."

With that, Eric sat down and wrote a short note on a piece of paper. He folded it carefully. Then Eric walked over to Miss Pim and talked to her for a few minutes. He pointed to the house and gave her special instructions.

Early the following Monday morning, Dr. Burdley, Eric and Beatrice returned to the Jim Thompson house. They had come to say good-bye. As they arrived, Mr. Wise was unlocking the house.

"Guards have been here all night. The blue and white vase was on the tall Chinese table when we locked the doors. No one could have moved the vase this time," he told everyone.

The group walked upstairs to the dining room. They all crowded through the door to look. The vase was gone again! Once more, it had been moved to the small cabinet.

"Impossible," said Mr. Wise. "This is truly impossible. How could anyone have done this?" he asked.

To everyone's surprise, Eric answered, "I know, and I will be able to tell you if you go with me to the café."

The group of astonished adults followed Eric downstairs to the café. Much to their surprise, they found Miss Pim talking to a very old lady. The lady had her gray hair tied back in a neat bun. She wore a long silk skirt and had a nice shawl wrapped around her shoulders.

When the group walked up to them, Miss Pim stood up and said, "I would like to introduce you to Madame Cham. She has a very interesting story to tell us."

Madame Cham turned to Mr. Wise and said, "Thank you for inviting me here. I wanted to speak with you."

"But I did not invite you here," replied Mr. Wise, looking extremely puzzled.

"I did," said Eric. "I wrote a note and asked Miss Pim to put it inside the blue and white vase after the last tour on Sunday night. The note said, 'Whoever is moving this vase to where Jim Thompson placed it, please come and meet me at the café on Monday morning.'"

"You have been moving the vase?" asked Mr. Wise in disbelief. "How did you get into the house?"

"I got into the house with the set of keys that unlock the little door in the back. Jim Thompson gave me the keys many years ago, and I have been coming here ever since. I come at five o'clock in the morning so I won't disturb the tours. I just row my little boat across the canal and enter through the gate in the garden," she replied.

Mr. Wise looked shocked, "I did not know there was a small door in the back of the house."

"Oh, the house has a secret door that only Jim Thompson and I knew about," she replied. "I remember this house from when it was still in our weaving village."

"But why have you been coming all
these years?" asked Miss Pim.

"You see, Jim Thompson was very kind
to my family. We wove silk for him and
made a good living. I was so grateful,
I wanted to do something for him. So,
I offered to dust off all his bowls and dishes.
I keep waiting for him to come back from his vacation. I want every
bowl to be as clean as on the day he left. But now I am getting old
and can only come once a week on Mondays," she explained.

"You have been very helpful. The dishes and bowls are always beautifully clean," said
Mr. Wise. "Thank you so much."

"I came today because I want to give you back the keys. I am too old and tired to
do this any more. Can you please find someone else to dust the bowls?" she asked.
Then Madame Cham handed the keys to Mr. Wise. She left without waiting for an
answer.

Mr. Wise looked at the keys in his hand and said, "Amazing, you have solved the mystery of the vanishing vase. But how did you figure it out?"

"Well, it was simple," said Eric. "I just put the clues together."

Eric explained: "My uncle told me the vase was very old and valuable. I wondered why a person who could move it did not try to steal it. Then I reasoned, this person must care about the vase and want it to be here. I also learned from the old photograph that the vase used to be on the little cabinet. Only someone who had been here for a long time would know this. That person must know things about this house that the rest of us do not know. He or she would also know a secret way to get into the house. So I decided if the person was honest and cared about the house, the simplest thing would be to ask him or her to come meet us."

"Brilliant!" said Mr. Wise. "This calls for a big reward. Ice cream and chocolate cake for Beatrice and Eric."

While they ate their ice cream and cake, Mr. Wise said, "You and Beatrice are two very smart young people. You must come back and visit us again."

"Oh, we would like to," said Beatrice. "We like this house. Every time we walk around, we discover new things."

Then Eric asked, "If we come back, do you think there will be another mystery for us to solve?"

"Oh, certainly," said Mr. Wise. "Your uncle, Dr. Burdley, will tell you that this museum is full of art treasures with many riddles and questions. And of course, the strangest mystery of all is what happened to Jim Thompson. Perhaps you can solve that next time!"

JIM THOMPSON

Jim Thompson, an American architect, was born in 1906 in Delaware. He first came to Thailand at the end of World War II. After deciding to make Bangkok his home, he started The Thai Silk Company with the help of friends. He very much appreciated Thai art and collected old Asian paintings, statues and ceramics. He disappeared mysteriously in 1967, while staying with friends in the Cameron Highlands of Malaysia. There are many theories about what happened to Jim Thompson, but no one really knows.